# TEACHER'S PET

**by Rita Walsh**
**illustrated by Chris Demarest**

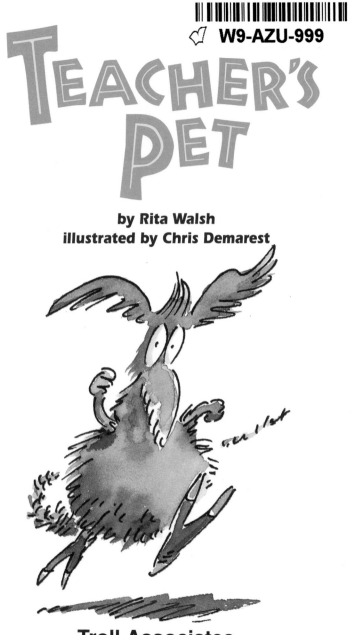

**Troll Associates**

Everyone knew that Mrs. Littlebirdy was weird. But no one guessed how strange she really was until the day she brought Fluffy to school.

It was the day of our school talent show. This year we all had to dress up as different presidents. I really wanted to be Abraham Lincoln, but Mrs. Littlebirdy made me Rutherford B. Hayes instead. I never even heard of Rutherford B. Hayes.

The teachers were supposed to
show off their talents, too.

Which meant another year of watching
Principal Dooley's lame rope tricks.

Everyone wondered what Mrs. Littlebirdy was going to do this year. Last year she entertained everyone with her imitations of different dinosaurs. She really scared the kindergartners when she did her Tyrannosaurus Rex.

We couldn't wait to see what was in store for us this year.

The class mothers arrived just after recess. Jessica's mom bounced into our classroom carrying a top hat and a fake beard. Jessica was going to be Honest Abe, which I thought was ridiculous since she was the shortest one in the class.

Mrs. Littlebirdy brought in a box with holes punched in the top.

"I thought I'd do an animal act with my little Fluffy," she said.

We all started getting into our costumes. I looked like a total dork.

But at least I didn't look as bad as Steve.
He had insisted on being Gerald Ford. Don't ask
me why.

While we were getting dressed, we heard some pretty strange noises coming from Fluffy's box. It sure didn't sound like a puppy or a kitten. In fact, it didn't sound like any animal I had ever heard.

Just then Heather started one of her sneezing bouts.

"My allergies!" she moaned.

"Oh, dear," said Mrs. Littlebirdy, shuffling Heather toward the door. "You must be allergic to Fluffy. We'd better get you down to Nurse Needleplenty right away."

We could hear Heather's sneezes echoing all the way down the hall.

"Oh, great," said Jessica, adjusting her beard. "Now who's going to be Dwight Eisenhower?"

We didn't have much time to think about it, though. Mr. DiBonanzo came in from next door and made us line up to go to the auditorium.

"What about Fluffy?" I asked. "Shouldn't he come to the auditorium, too?"

"President Fluffy?" said Mr. DiBonanzo.
"Hmmm, I don't remember him. Whoever is
President Fluffy, just get somewhere in line."
I reached over and picked up Fluffy's box.

We were supposed to go on right after the third grade finished their song about tooth brushing and flossing. They were lined up onstage in the shape of a big mouth, weaving a rope in and out.

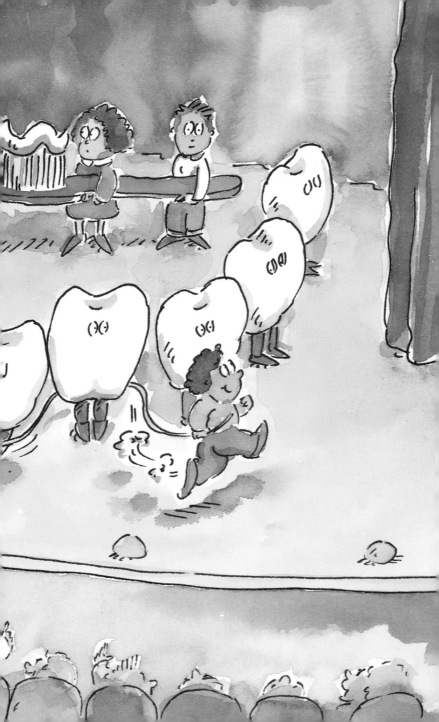

Steve walked up to me in the middle of the song.

"Hey, let's see the pooch," he whispered. "Open up the box."

So I did.

I dropped the box and screamed. Fluffy was no dog. He was a MONSTER! I don't know how Mrs. Littlebirdy managed to squish him into that box, but I could tell he wasn't going back in.

Jessica took one look at Fluffy and started to cry, which wasn't very dignified for Abraham Lincoln, if you ask me.

Alex was much more brave. "Heeeere, Fluffy," he said softly. "Here, boy."

He held the box open and walked toward Fluffy.

But Fluffy wasn't fooled. He grabbed one of the curtain ropes and climbed up to the top. Then he gave a loud holler and swooped down to the stage, crashing into a third grader dressed as a molar.

Principal Dooley leaped onto the stage.
He swung a lasso over his head and shouted,
"Yippee-ki-yi-yay!"

Of course, the rope didn't land anywhere near Fluffy.

Janitor Moppinshine tried to corner Fluffy in the orchestra pit. Fluffy slid across the shiny top of the piano and leaped to center stage.

Jessica turned to her mother. "I wanna go home!" she whined, throwing her hat and beard on the floor.

Some Abraham Lincoln she was! She and her mother ran out the fire door.

The rest of us formed a big circle to surround Fluffy. The PTA president grabbed a fire extinguisher.

Fluffy began to whimper. He knew he was trapped. Alex opened the box and the monster crept back in, his long straggly tail tucked under him.

Just then Mrs. Littlebirdy and Heather rushed backstage. From the looks of Heather, her allergy doctor was going to be busy for a long time.

"Are we all ready to go on?" Mrs. Littlebirdy asked breathlessly.

I picked up Jessica's costume. I stood as tall as I could. "Four score and seven years ago..." I murmured.

It looked like I was going to be Abraham Lincoln after all. Thanks, Fluffy!